Robert Blair

The Grave

Robert Blair

The Grave

ISBN/EAN: 9783744716338

Printed in Europe, USA, Canada, Australia, Japan

Cover: Foto ©Andreas Hilbeck / pixelio.de

More available books at **www.hansebooks.com**

THE

GRAVE.

A

POEM.

By ROBERT BLAIR,

The House appointed for all Living. Job.

The EIGHTH EDITION.

LONDON,

Printed for G. ROBINSON, Pater-noster Row, 1776.

[Price Six-Pence.]

THE
GRAVE.
A
POEM.

WHILST some affect the sun, and some the shade,
Some flee the city; some the hermitage,
Their arms as various, as the roads they take
In journeying thro' life; the task be mine,
To paint the gloomy horrors of the *tomb*:
The appointed place of rendezvous, where all
These travellers meet. Thy succours I implore,
Eternal King! whose potent arm sustains
The keys of hell and death.——The Grave; dread thing!
Men shiver when thou'rt nam'd: Nature appall'd,
Shakes off her wonted firmness. Ah! how dark,

Thy

Thy long extended realms, and rueful waftes !

Where nought but filence reigns, and night, dark night,

Dark as was Chaos, 'ere the infant fun

Was roll'd together, or had try'd its beams

Athwart the gloom profound ! The fickly taper

By glimmering thro' thy low-brow'd mifty vaults,

(Furr'd round with mouldy damps, and ropy flime,)

Lets fall a fupernumerary horror;

And only ferves to make thy night more irkfome.

Well do I know thee by thy trufty yew,

Chearlefs, unfocial plant! that loves to dwell

'Midft fculls and coffins, epitaphs and worms:

Where light-heel'd ghofts, and vifionary fhades,

Beneath the wan cold moon (as fame reports)

Embody'd thick, perform their myftick rounds.

No other merriment, dull tree ! is thine.

See yonder hallow'd fane! the pious work

Of names once fam'd, now dubious or forgot,

And buried 'midft the wreck of things which were:

There lie interr'd the more illuftrious dead.

The wind is up : hark ! how it howls ! methinks

Till

Till now, I never heard a found fo dreary:
Doors creek, and windows clap, and Night's foul bird
Rook'd in the fpire fcreams loud: the gloomy aifles
Black-plafter'd, and hung round with fhreds of fcutcheons
And tatter'd coats of arms, fend back the found
Laden with heavier airs, from the low vaults
The manfions of the dead. Rouz'd from their flumbers
In grim array the grizly fpectres rife,
Grin horrible, and obftinately fullen
Pafs and repafs, hufh'd as the foot of Night.
Again! the fcreech-owl fhrieks: ungracious found!
I'll hear no more, it makes one's blood run chill.

Quite round the pile, a row of reverend elms,
Cœval near with that, all ragged fhew,
Long lafh'd by the rude winds: fome rift half down
Their branchlefs trunks: others fo thin a top,
That fcarce two crows could lodge in the fame tree.
Strange things, the neighbours fay, have happen'd here
Wild fhrieks have iffued from the hollow tombs,
Dead men have come again, and walk'd about,
And the great bell has toll'd, unrung, untouch'd.

(Such

(Such tales their cheer, at wake or goſſiping,
When it draws near to witching-time of night.)

Oft in the lone church-yard at night I've ſeen
By glimpſe of moon-ſhine, chequering thro' the trees,
The ſchool-boy with his ſatchel in his hand,
Whiſtling aloud to bear his courage up,
And lightly tripping o'er the long flat ſtones
(With nettles ſkirted, and with moſs o'ergrown,)
That tell in homely phraſe who lie below;
Sudden! he ſtarts, and hears, or thinks he hears
The ſound of ſomething purring at his heels:
Full faſt he flies, and dares not look behind him,
Till out of breath he overtakes his fellows:
Who gather round and wonder at the tale
Of horrid apparition, tall and ghaſtly,
That walks at dead of night, or takes his ſtand
O'er ſome new open'd Grave; and, ſtrange to tell!
Evaniſhes at crowing of the cock.

The new-made widow too, I've ſometimes ſpy'd,
Sad ſight! ſlow moving o'er the proſtrate dead:
Liſtleſs, ſhe crawls along in doleful black;

Whilſt burſts of ſorrow guſh from either eye,
Faſt-falling down her now untaſted cheek,
Prone on the lowly grave of the dear man
She drops; whilſt buſy-meddling Memory,
In barbarous ſucceſſion, muſters up
The paſt endearments of their ſofter hours,
Tenacious of its theme. Still, ſtill ſhe thinks
She ſees him, and indulging the fond thought,
Clings yet more cloſely to the ſenſeleſs turf,
Nor heeds the paſſenger who looks that way.

Invidious Grave! how do'ſt thou rend in ſunder
Whom love has knit, and ſympathy made one;
A tie more ſtubborn far than nature's band!
Friendſhip! myſterious cement of the ſoul,
Sweetener of life, and ſolder of ſociety,
I owe thee much. Thou haſt deſerv'd from me,
Far, far beyond what I can ever pay.
Oft have I prov'd the labours of thy love,
And the warm efforts of the gentle heart
Anxious to pleaſe. Oh! when my friend and I
In ſome thick wood have wander'd heedleſs on,

Hid

Hid from the vulgar eye; and fat us down

Upon the floping cowflip-cover'd bank,

Where the pure limpid ftream has flid along

In grateful errors thro' the under-wood

Sweet murmuring: methought, the fhrill-tongu'd thrufh

Mended his fong of love; the footy blackbird

Mellow'd his pipe, and foften'd ev'ry note:

The eglantine fmell'd fweeter, and the rofe

Affum'd a dye more deep; whilft ev'ry flower

Vy'd with its fellow-plant in luxury

Of drefs. Oh! then the longeft fummer's day

Seem'd too, too much in hafte: ftill the full heart

Had not imparted half: 'twas happinefs

Too exquifite to laft. Of joys departed

Not to return, how painful the remembrance!

Dull Grave: thou fpoil'ft the dance of youthful blood,

Strik'ft out the dimple from the cheek of mirth,

And ev'ry fmirking feature from the face;

Branding our laughter with the name of madnefs.

Where are the jefters now? the men of health

Complexionally pleafant? where the droll

Whofe.

Whofe ev'ry look and gefture was a joke
To clapping theatres and fhouting crouds,
And made even thick-lip'd mufing Melancholy
To gather up her face into a fmile
Before fhe was aware? Ah! fullen now,
And dumb as the green turf that covers them!

Where are the mighty thunderbolts of war?
The Roman Cæfars, and the Græcian chiefs,
The boaft of ftory? Where the hot-brain'd youth?
Who the tiara at his pleafure tore
From kings of all the then difcover'd globe;
And cry'd forfooth, becaufe his arm was hamper'd,
And had not room enough to do its work?
Alas! how flim, difhonourably flim!
And cramm'd into a fpace we blufh to name.
Proud royalty! how alter'd in thy looks?
How blank thy features, and how wan thy hue?
Son of the morning! whither art thou gone?
Where haft thou hid thy many-fpangled head,
And the majeftic menace of thine eyes
Felt from afar? pliant and powerlefs now,

B   Like

Like new-born infant wound up in his swathes,
Or victim tumbled flat upon his back
That throbs beneath the sacrificer's knife:
Mute, must thou bear the strife of little tongues,
And coward insults of the base-born crowd;
That grudge a privilege thou never hadst,
But only hop'd for in the peaceful Grave,
Of being unmolested and alone.
Arabia's gums and odoriferous drugs,
And honours by the heralds duly paid
In mode and form, ev'n to a very scruple,
Oh cruel irony! these come too late;
And only mock, whom they were meant to honour,
Surely, there's not a dungeon slave that's bury'd
In the highway, unshrouded and uncoffin'd,
But lies as soft, and sleeps as sound as he,
Sorry pre-eminence, of high descent,
Above the vulgar-born, to rot in state.

But see! the well-plum'd hearse comes nodding on
Stately and slow; and properly attended
By the whole sable tribe, that painful watch

The

The fick man's door, and live upon the dead,

By letting out their perfons by the hour

To mimick forrow, when the heart's not fad.

How rich the trappings, now they're all unfurl'd,

And glittering in the fun! triumphant entries

Of conquerors, and coronation pomps,

In glory fcarce exceed. Great gluts of people

Retard th' unweildy fhew; whilft from the cafements

And houfes tops, ranks behind ranks clofe-wedg'd

Hang bellying o'er. But! tell us, why this wafte?

Why this ado in earthing up a carcafe

That's fall'n into difgrace, and in the noftril

Smells horrible? Ye undertakers! tell us,

'Midft all the gorgeous figures you exhibit,

Why is the principal concealed, for which

You make this mighty ftir? 'Tis wifely done:

What would offend the eye in a good picture,

The painter cafts difcreetly into fhades.

    Proud lineage! now how little thou appear'ft

Below the envy of the private man!

Honour! that meddlefome officious ill,

Purfues

Purfues thee ev'n to death; nor there ftops fhort;
Strange perfecution! when the Grave itfelf
Is no protection from rude fufferance.

Abfurd! to think to over-reach the Grave,
And from the wreck of names to refcue ours!
The beft concerted fchemes men lay for fame
Die faft away: only themfelves die fafter.
The far-fam'd fculptor, and the laurell'd bard,
Thofe bold infurances of deathlefs fame,
Supply their little feeble aids in vain.
The tap'ring pyramid, th' Egyptian's pride,
And wonder of the world, whofe fpiky top
Has wounded the thick cloud, and long outliv'd
The angry fhaking of the winter's ftorm:
Yet fpent at laft by the injuries of heaven,
Shatter'd with age, and furrow'd o'er with years,
The myftic cone with hieroglyphics crefted
Gives way. Oh lamentable fight! at once
The labour of whole ages lumbers down;
A heideous and mifhapen length of ruins,
Sepulchral columns wreftle but in vain

With

With all-fubduing Time: his cank'ring hand
With calm deliberate malice wafteth them:
Worn on the edge of days, the brafs confumes,
The bufto moulders, and the deep cut marble,
Unfteady to the fteel, gives up its charge,
Ambition, half convicted of her folly,
Hangs down the head, and reddens at the tale.

Here all the mighty troublers of the earth,
Who fwarm to fov'reign rule thro' feas of blood;
Th' oppreffive, fturdy, man-deftroying villains,
Who ravag'd kingdoms, and laid empires wafte,
And in a cruel wantonnefs of power
Thinn'd ftates of half their people, and gave up
To want the reft: now like a ftorm that's fpent,
Lie hufh'd, and meanly fneak behind thy covert.
Vain thought! to hide them from the general fcorn,
That haunts and dogs them like an injur'd ghoft
Implacable. Here too the petty tyrant
Of fcant domains, geographer ne'er notic'd,
And well for neighb'ring grounds, of arm as fhort:
Who fix'd his iron talons on the poor,

And

And grip'd them like fome lordly beaft of prey;
Deaf to the forceful cries of gnawing hunger,
And piteous plaintive voice of Mifery :
(As if a flave was not a fhred of nature,
Of the fame common nature with his lord :)
Now, tame and humble, like a child that's whipp'd
Shakes hands with duft, and calls the worm his kinfman,
Nor pleads his rank and birthright. Under ground
Precedency's a jeft; vaffal and lord
Grofly familiar, fide by fide confume.

When felf efteem, or others adulation,
Would cunningly perfuade us we are fomething
Above the common level of our kind :
The grave gainfays the fmooth-complexion'd flatt'ry,
And with blunt truth acquaints us what we are.

Beauty ! thou pretty play-thing, dear deceit,
That fteals fo foftly o'er the ftripling's heart,
And gives it a new pulfe, unknown before,
The Grave difcredits thee : Thy charms expung'd,
Thy rofes faded, and thy lillies foil'd;

What

What haſt thou more to boaſt of? Will thy lovers
Flock round thee now, to gaze and do thee homage?
Methinks, I ſee thee with thy head low laid;
Whilſt ſurfeited upon thy damaſk cheek,
The high-fed worm, in lazy volumes roll'd,
Riots unſcar'd.　For this was all thy caution?
For this, thy painful labours at thy glaſs?
T'improve thoſe charms, and keep them in repair,
For which the ſpoiler thanks thee not.　Foul-feeder!
Coarſe fare and carrion pleaſe thee full as well,
And leave as keen a reliſh on the ſenſe.
Look, how the fair one weeps! the conſcious tears
Stand thick as dew-drops on the bells of flowers:
Honeſt effuſion! the ſwoln heart in vain
Works hard to put a gloſs on its diſtreſs.

　Strength too! thou ſurly, and leſs gentle boaſt
Of thoſe that laugh loud at the village ring,
A fit of common ſickneſs pulls thee down
With greater eaſe, than e'er thou didſt the ſtripling
That raſhly dar'd thee to the unequal fight.
What groan was that I heard? deep groan indeed!

With

With anguiſh heavy-laden; let me trace it:
From yonder bed it comes, where the ſtrong man,
By ſtronger arm belabour'd, gaſps for breath
Like a hard-hunted beaſt, How his great heart
Beats thick! his roomy cheſt by far too ſcant
To give the lungs full play! what now avail
The ſtrong-built ſinewy limbs, and well ſpread ſhoulders?
See! how he tugs for life, and lays about him,
Mad with his pain! eager he catches hold
Of what comes next to hand, and graſps it hard,
Juſt like a creature drowning, hideous ſight!
Oh, how his eyes ſtand out! and ſtare full ghaſtly,
Whilſt the diſtemper's rank and deadly venom
Shoots like a burning arrow croſs his bowels,
And drinks his marrow up. Hear you that groan?
It was his laſt. See how the great Goliah,
Juſt like a child that brawl'd itſelf to reſt,
Lies ſtill, What mean'ſt thou then, O mighty boaſter,
To vaunt of nerves of thine? What means the bull,
Unconſcious of his ſtrength, to play the coward,
And flee before a feeble thing like man;

That

That knowing well the flackneſs of his arm,
Truſts only in the well invented knife?

With ſtudy pale, and midnight vigils ſpent,
The ſtar-ſurveying ſage, cloſe to his eye
Applies the ſight-invigorating tube;
And travelling through the boundleſs length of ſpace,
Marks well the courſes of the far ſeen orbs,
That roll with regular confuſion there,
In extaſy of thought. But ah! proud man,
Great heights are hazardous to the weak head:
Soon, very ſoon, thy firmeſt footing fails;
And down thou dropp'ſt into that darkſome place,
Where nor device, or knowledge ever came.

Here, the tongue-warrior lies, diſabled now,
Diſarm'd, diſhonour'd like a wretch that's gagg'd,
And cannot tell his ail to paſſers by.
Great man of language! whence this mighty change?
This dumb deſpair, and drooping of the head?
Tho' ſtrong Perſuaſion hung upon thy lip,
And ſly Inſinuation's ſofter arts

C

In ambuſh lay about thy flowing tongue;
Alas how chop-fallen now? thick miſts and ſilence
Reſt like a weary cloud, upon thy breaſt
Unceaſing. Ah! where is the lifted arm,
The ſtrength of action and the force of words,
The well-turn'd period, and the well-tun'd voice;
With all the leſſer ornaments of phraſe?
Ah! fled for ever, as they ne'er had been!
Raz'd from the book of fame: or more provoking,
Perchance ſome hackney hunger-bitten ſcribler
Inſults thy memory, and blots thy tomb
With long flat narrative, or duller rhimes
With heavy-halting pace that drawl along;
Enough to rouſe a dead man into rage,
And warm with red reſentment the wan cheek.

Here, the great maſters of the healing art,
Theſe mighty mock-defrauders of the tomb!
Spite of their juleps and catholicons
Reſign to fate. Proud Æſculapius' ſon,
Where are thy boaſted implements of art,
And all thy well-cramm'd magazines of health?

Nor hill, nor vale, as far as ſhip could go,

Nor margin of the gravel-bottom'd brook,

Eſcap'd thy rifling hand: from ſtubborn ſhrubs

Thou wrung'ſt their ſhy retiring virtues out,

And vex'd them in the fire; nor fly, nor infect,

Nor writhy ſnake, eſcap'd thy deep reſearch.

But why this apparatus? why this coſt?

Tell us, thou doughty keeper from the grave!

Where are thy recipes and cordials now,

With the long liſt of vouchers for thy cures?

Alas! thou ſpeakeſt not. The bold impoſtor

Looks not more ſilly, when the cheat's found out.

Here, the lank-ſided miſer, worſt of felons!

Who meanly ſtole, diſcreditable ſhift!

From back and belly too, their proper cheer;

Eas'd of a tax, it irk'd the wretch to pay

To his own carcaſs, now lies cheaply lodg'd,

By clam'rous appetites no longer teaz'd,

Nor tedious bills of charges and repairs.

But ah! where are his rents, his comings in?

Ay! now you have made the rich man poor indeed:

Robb'd

Robb'd of his Gods, what has he left behind !
Oh, curfed luft of gold! when for thy fake
The fool throws up his int'reft in both worlds,
Firft ftarv'd in this, than damn'd in that to come.

How fhocking muft the fummons be, O death !
To him that is at eafe in his poffeffions;
Who counting on long years of pleafure here,
Is quite unfurnifh'd for that world to come !
In that dread moment, how the frantick foul
Raves round the walls of her clay tenement,
Runs to each avenue, and fhrieks for help,
But fhrieks in vain! how wifhfully fhe looks
On all fhe's leaving, now no longer hers!
A little longer, yet a little longer.
Oh, might fhe ftay to wafh away her ftains,
And fit her for her paffage! mournful fight!
Her very eyes weep blood; and every groan
She heaves is big with horror: but the foe,
Like a ftanch murth'rer fteady to his purpofe
Purfues her clofe through ev'ry lane of life,
Nor miffes once the track, but preffes on ;

Till

Till forc'd at laſt to the tremendous verge,
At once ſhe ſinks to everlaſting ruin.

Sure, 'tis a ſerious thing to die! my ſoul!
What a ſtrange moment muſt it be, when near
Thy journey's end, thou haſt the gulf in view?
That awful gulf, no mortal e'er repaſs'd
To tell what's doing on the other ſide!
Nature runs back, and ſhudders at the ſight,
And every life-ſtring bleeds at thoughts of parting!
For part they muſt: body and ſoul muſt part;
Fond couple! link'd more cloſe than wedded pair.
This wings its way to its Almighty ſource,
The witneſs of its actions, now its judge;
That drops into the dark and noiſome grave,
Like a diſabled pitcher of no uſe,

If death was nothing, and nought after death;
If when men dy'd, at once they ceas'd to be,
Returning to the barren womb of nothing
Whence firſt they ſprung; then might the debauchee
Untrembling mouth the heav'ns: then might the drunkard
Reel over his full bowl, and when 'tis drain'd,

Fill

Fill up another to the brim, and laugh

At the poor bug-bear death: then might the wretch

That's weary of the world, and tir'd of life,

At once give each inquietude the flip

By ftealing out of being, when he pleas'd,

And by what way; whether by hemp or fteel:

Death's thoufand doors ftand open. Who could force

The ill-pleas'd gueft to fit out his full time,

Or blame him if he goes? Sure he does well

That helps himfelf as timely as he can,

When able. But if there is an hereafter,

And that there is, confcience, uninfluenc'd

And fuffered to fpeak out, tells ev'ry man:

Then muft it be an awful thing to die:

More horrid yet, to die by one's own hand.

Self-murther! name it not: our ifland's fhame:

That makes her the reproach of neighbouring ftates.

Shall nature, fwerving from her earlieft dictate

Self-prefervation, fall by her own act?

Forbid it heaven! let not upon difguft

The fhamelefs hand be foully crimfon'd o'er

With

With blood of its own lord. Dreadful attempt!
Juſt reeking from ſelf-ſlaughter, in a rage
To ruſh into the preſence of our judge!
As if we challeng'd him to do his worſt,
And matter'd not his wrath. Unheard of tortures
Muſt be reſerv'd for ſuch: theſe herd together;
The common damn'd ſhun their ſociety,
And look upon themſelves as fiends leſs foul.
Our time is fix'd, and all our days are number'd;
How long, how ſhort, we know not: this we know,
Duty requires we calmly wait the ſummons,
Nor dare to ſtir ſtill heav'n ſhall give permiſſion:
Like centries that muſt keep their deſtin'd ſtand,
And wait th' appointed hour, till they are reliev'd.
Thoſe only are the brave, who keep their ground,
And keep it to the laſt. To run away
Is but a coward's trick: to run away
From this world's ills, that at the very worſt
Will ſoon blow o'er, thinking to mend ourſelves
By boldly vent'ring on a world unknown,
And plunging headlong in the dark; 'tis mad:
No frenzy half ſo deſperate as this.

Tell

Tell us ye dead! will none of you in pity
To thofe you left behind difclofe the fecret?
Oh that fome courteous ghoft would blab it out!
What 'tis you are, and we muft fhortly be.
I've heard, that fouls departed have fometimes
Forewarn'd men of their death: 'twas kindly done
To knock and give th' alarm.   But what means
This ftinted charity? 'tis but lame kindnefs
That does its work by halves.   Why might you not
Tell us what 'tis to die? Do the ftrict laws
Of your fociety forbid your fpeaking
Upon a point fo nice? I'll afk no more:
Sullen, like lamps in fepulchres, your fhine
Enlightens but yourfelves: well —'tis no matter;
A very little time will clear up all,
And make us learn'd as you are, and as clofe.

Death's fhafts fly thick. Here falls the village fwain,
And there his pamper'd lord.   The cup goes round;
And who fo artful as to put it by?
'Tis long fince death had the majority;
Yet ftrange! the living lay it not to heart.

See

See yonder maker of the dead man's bed;

The fexton! hoary-headed chronicle,

Of hard unmeaning face, down which ne'er ftole

A gentle tear; with mattock in his hand

Digs through whole rows of kindred and acquaintance;

By far his juniors! fcarce a fcull's caft up,

But well he knew its owner, and can tell

Some paffage of his life.   Thus hand in hand

The fot has walk'd with Death twice twenty years;

And yet ne'er yonker on the green laughs louder,

Or clubs a fmuttier tale: when drunkards meet,

None fings a merrier catch, or lends a hand

More willing to his cup.   Poor wretch! he minds not,

That foon fome trufty brother of the trade

Shall do for him what he has done for thoufands.

On this fide, and on that, men fee their friends

Drop off, like leaves in autumn; yet launch out

Into fantaftic fchemes, which the long livers

In the world's hale and undegen'rate days,

Could fcarce have leafure for.   Fools that we are!

Never to think of Death and of Ourfelves

At

At the fame time! as if to learn to die

Were no concern of ours. Oh more than fottifh!

For creatures of a day, in gamefome mood

To frolick on eternity's dread brink,

Unapprehenfive; when for ought we know

The very firft fwoln furge fhall fweep us in.

Think we, or think we not, time hurries on

With a refiftlefs unremitting ftream,

Yet treads more foft than e'er did midnight thief,

That flides his hand under the mifer's pillow,

And carries off his prize. What is this world?

What! but a fpacious burial-field unwall'd,

Strew'd with death's fpoils, the fpoils of animals

Savage and tame, and full of dead men's bones.

The very turf on which we tread, once liv'd;

And we that live muft lend our carcafes

To cover our own offspring: in their turns

They too muft cover theirs. 'Tis here all meet:

The fhiv'ring Icelander, and fun-burnt Moor;

Men of climes, that never met before;

And of all creeds, the Jew, the Turk, and Chriftian:

Here the proud prince, and favourite yet prouder,

His

His fov'reign's keeper, and the people's fcourge,

Are huddled out of fight.   Here lie abafh'd

The great negotiators of the earth,

And celebrated mafters of the ballance,

Deep read in ftratagems, and wiles of courts:

Now vain their treaty-fkill, death fcorns to treat.

Here the o'erloaded flave flings down his burthen

From his gall'd fhoulders; and when the cruel tyrant,

With all his guards and tools of pow'r about him,

Is meditating new unheard-of harfhips,

Mocks his fhort arm, and quick as thought efcapes

Where tyrants vex not, and the weary reft.

Here the warm lover, leaving the cool fhade,

The tell-tale echo, and the bubbling ftream,

(Time out of mind the fav'rite feats of love,)

Faft by his gentle miftrefs lays him down

Unblafted by foul tongue.   Here friends and foes

Lie clofe; unmindful of their former feuds.

The lawn-rob'd prelate, and plain prefbyter,

E'er while that ftood aloof, as fhy to meet,

Familiar mingle here, like fifter-ftreams

That fome rude interpofing rock had fplit.

Here

Here is the large-lim'd peafant: here the child
Of a fpan long, that never faw the fun,
Nor pref,'d the nipple, ftrangled in life's porch :
Here is the mother with her fons and daughters ;
The barren wife ; and long-demurring maid,
Whofe lonely unappropriated fweets
Smil'd like yon knot of cowflips on the cliff,
Not to be come at by the willing hand.
Here are the prude fevere, and gay coquent,
The fober widow, and the young green virgin,
Cropp'd like a rofe, before 'tis fully blown,
Or half its worth difclos'd.   Strange medley here !
Here garrulous old age winds up his tale;
And jovial youth of lightfome vacant heart,
Whofe ev'ry day was made of melody,
Hears not the voice of mirth : the fhrill-tongu'd fhrew,
Meek as the turtle dove, forgets her chiding.
Here are the wife, the generous and the brave ;
The juft, the good, the worthlefs, the prophane,
The downright clown, and perfectly well-bred ;
The fool, the churl, the fcoundrel, and the mean,
The fupple ftatefman and the patriot ftern;

The

The wrecks of nations, and the spoils of time,
With all the lumber of six thousand years.

　　Poor man ! how happy once in thy first state!
When yet but warm from thy great Maker's hand,
He stamp'd thee with his image, and well pleased
Smil'd on his last fair work.　Then all was well.
Sound was the body, and the soul serene;
Like two sweet instruments ne'er out of tune,
That play their several parts.　Nor head, nor heart,
Offer'd to ache : nor was there cause they should;
For all was pure within : no fell remorse,
Nor anxious castings up of what might be,
Alarm'd his peaceful bosom : summer seas
Shew not more smooth, when kiss'd by southern winds,
Just ready to expire.　Scarce importun'd,
The generous soil with a luxuriant hand
Offer'd the various produce of the year,
And every thing most perfect in its kind.
Blessed ! thrice blessed days ! but ah, how short!
Bless'd as the pleasing dreams of holy men ;
But fugitive like those, and quickly gone.
　　　　　　　　　　　　　　　　Oh,

Oh, flipp'ry ftate of things! what fudden turns?

What ftrange viciffitudes, in the firft leaf

Of man's fad hiftory? to-day moft happy,

And 'ere to-morrow's fun has fet, moft abject!

How fcant the fpace between thefe vaft extremes!

Thus far'd it with our Sire: Not long he enjoy'd

His paradife! fcarce had the happy tenant

Of the fair fpot due time to prove its fweets,

Or fum them up; when ftrait he muft be gone

Ne'er to return again. And muft he go?

Can nought compound for the firft dire offence

Of erring man? Like one that is condemn'd,

Fain would he trifle time with idle talk,

And parley with his fate. But 'tis in vain.

Not all the lavifh odours of the place

Offer'd in incenfe can procure his pardon,

Or mitigate his doom. A mighty angel

With flaming fword forbids his longer ftay,

And drives the loiterer forth; nor muft he take

One laft and farewell round. At once he loft

His glory, and his God. If mortal now,

And forely maim'd, no wonder! Man has finn'd.

Sick

Sick of his blifs, and bent on new adventures,

Evil he wou'd needs try: nor try'd in vain.

(Dreadful experiment! deftructive meafure!

Where the worft thing could happen, was fuccefs)

Alas! too well he fped: the good he fcorn'd

Stalk'd off reluctant, like an ill-us'd ghoft,

Not to return; or if it did, its vifits

Like thofe of angels fhort, and far between:

Whilft the black dæmon with his hell-fcap'd train,

Admitted once into its better room,

Grew loud and mutinous, nor would be gone;

Lording it o'er the man, who now too late

Saw the rafh error, which he could not mend:

An error fatal not to him alone,

But to his future fons, his fortune's heirs.

Inglorious bondage! human nature groans

Beneath a vaffalage fo vile and cruel,

And its vaft body bleeds at ev'ry pore.

What havock haft thou made? foul monfter, fin!

Greateft and firft of ills! the fruitful parent

Of woes of all dimenfions! but for thee

Sorrow

Sorrow had never been. All noxious things,
Of vileft nature! Other forts of evils
Are kindly circumfcrib'd, and have their bounds.
The fierce volcano, from its burning entrails
That belches molten ftone and globes of fire,
Involv'd in pitchy clouds of fmoke and ftench,
Marrs the adjacent fields for fome leagues round,
And there it ftops. The big-fwoln inundation,
Of mifchief more diffufive; raving loud,
Buries whole tracts of country, threat'ning more;
But that too has its fhore it cannot pafs.
More dreadful far than thefe! fin has laid wafte
Not here and there a country, but a world:
Difpatching at a wide extended blow
Entire mankind; and for their fakes defacing
A whole creation's beauty with rude hands;
Blafting the foodful grain, the loaded branches,
And marking all along its way with ruin.
Accurfed thing! oh, where fhall fancy find
A proper name to call thee by, expreffive
Of all thy horrors? pregnant womb of ills
Of temper fo tranfcendently malign,

That

That toads and ferpents of moft deadly kind
Compar'd to thee are harmlefs. Sickneffes
of ev'ry fize and fymptom, racking pains,
And blueft plagues are thine! See how the fiend
Profufely fcatters the contagion round!
Whilft deep-mouth'd flaughter bellowing at her heels
Wades deep in blood new fpilt; yet for to-morrow
Shapes out new work of great uncommon daring,
And inly pines till the dread blow is ftruck.

But hold! I've gone too far; too much difcover'd
My father's nakednefs, and nature's fhame.
Here let me paufe! and drop an honeft tear,
One burft of filial duty, and condolance,
O'er all thofe ample deferts death hath fpread,
This chaos of mankind. O great man-eater!
Whofe ev'ry day is carnival, not fated yet!
Unheard-of epicure! without a fellow!
The verieft gluttons do not always cram;
Some intervals of abftinence are fought
To edge the appetite: thou feekeft none.
Methinks the countlefs fwarms thou haft devour'd

E

And

And thoufands that each hour thou gobbleft up;
This, lefs than this, might gorge thee to the full!
But ah! rapacious ftill, thou gap'ft for more:
Like one, whole days defrauded of his meals,
On whom lank hunger lays his fkinny hand,
And whets to keeneft eagernefs his cravings,
(As if difeafes, maffacres, and poifon,
Famine, and war, were not thy caterers!)

But know that thou muft render up thy dead,
And with high int'reft too! they are not thine;
But only in thy keeping for a feafon,
Till the great promis'd day of reftitution;
When loud diffufive found from brazen trump
Of ftrong-lung'd cherub fhall alarm thy captives,
And roufe the long, long fleepers into life,
Day-light, and liberty.————————
Then muft thy gates fly open, and reveal
The mines, that lay long forming under ground,
In their dark cells immur'd: but now full ripe,
And pure as filver from the crucible,
That twice has ftood the torture of the fire

And

And inquifition of the forge. We know,
Th' illuftrious deliverer of mankind,
THE SON OF GOD, thee foil'd. Him in thy pow'r
Thou couldft not hold : felf-vigorous he rofe,
And fhaking off thy fetters, foon retook
Thofe fpoils his voluntary yielding lent.
(Sure pledge of our releafement from thy thrall ;)
Twice twenty days he fojourn'd here on earth,
And fhew'd himfelf alive to chofen witneffes
By proofs fo ftrong that the moft flow affenting
Had not a fcruple left. This having done,
He mounted up to Heav'n. Methinks ! I fee him
Climb the aerial heights, and glide along
Athwart the fevering clouds : but the faint eye
Flung backwards in the chace, foon drops its hold ;
Difabled quite, and jaded with purfuing.
Heaven's portals wide expand to let him in ;
Nor are his friends fhut out : as fome great prince
Not for himfelf alone procures admiffion,
But for his train : it was his royal will,
That where he is, there fhould his followers be.
Death only lies between ; a gloomy path !

Made

Made yet more gloomy by our coward fears!

But not untrod, nor tedious: the fatigue

Will soon go off. Besides, there's no by-road

To bliss. Then why, like ill-condition'd children,

Start we at transient hardships, in the way

That leads to purer air, and softer skies,

And a ne'er-setting sun? Fools that we are!

We wish to be where sweets unwith'ring bloom;

But strait our wish revoke, and will not go.

So have I seen upon a summer's even,

Fast by the riv'let's brink, a youngster play:

How wishfully he looks to stem the tide,

This moment resolute, next unresolv'd:

At last, he dips his foot; but as he dips,

His fears redouble, and he runs away

From th' inoffensive stream, unmindful now

Of all the flow'rs that paint the further bank,

And smil'd so sweet of late. Thrice welcome death!

That after many a painful bleeding step

Conducts us to our home, and lands us safe

On the long-wish'd for shore. Prodigious change!

Our bane turn'd to a blessing! death disarm'd

Loses

Lofes his fellnefs quite.   All thanks to him

Who fcourg'd the venom out.   Sure! the laft end

Of the good man is peace.   How calm his exit!

Night dews fall not more gently to the ground,

Nor weary worn-out winds expire fo foft,

Behold him! in the evening-tide of life,

A life well-fpent, whofe early care it was

His riper years fhould not upbraid his green :

By unperceiv'd degrees he wears away ;

Yet like the fun feems larger at his fetting!

High in his faith and hopes, look! how he reaches

After the prize in view! and like a bird

That's hamper'd, ftruggles hard to get away!

Whilft the glad gates of fight are wide expanded

To let new glories in, the firft fair fruits

Of the faft-coming harveft.   Then! oh then!

Each earth-born joy grows vile, or difappears,

Shrunk to a thing of nought.   Oh! how he longs

To have his pafsport fign'd, and be difmifs'd!

'Tis done ; and now he's happy: the glad foul

Has not a wifh uncrown'd.   Ev'n the lag flefh

Refts too in hope of meeting once again

Its

Its better half, never to funder more.

Nor fhall it hope in vain : the time draws on

When not a fingle fpot of burial-earth,

Whether on land, or in the fpacious fea,

But muft give back its long committed duft

Inviolate : and faithfully fhall thefe

Make up the full account ; not the leaft atom

Embezzl'd, or miflaid, of the whole tale.

Each foul fhall have a body ready furnifh'd ;

And each fhall have his own.   Hence ye prophane !

Afk not, how this can be ? Sure the fame pow'r

That rear'd the piece at firft, and took it down,

Can re-affemble the loofe fcatter'd parts,

And put them as they were.   Almighty God

Has done much more ; nor is his arm impair'd

Thro' length of days ; and what he can, he will :

His faithfulnefs ftands bound to fee it done.

When the dread trumpet founds, the flumb'ring duft,

Not unattentive to the call, fhall wake :

And ev'ry joint poffefs its proper place,

With a new elegance of form, unknown

To its firft ftate.   Nor fhall the confcious foul

Miftake

Miſtake its partner; but amidſt the croud
Singling its other half, into its arms
Shall ruſh, with all th' impatience of a man
That's new-come home, who having long been abſent
With haſte runs over ev'ry different room,
In pain to ſee the whole. Thrice happy meeting!
Nor time, nor death, ſhall ever part them more.

'Tis but a night, a long and moonleſs night,
We make the grave our bed, and then are gone.

Thus at the ſhut of ev'n, the weary bird
Leaves the wide air, and in ſome lonely brake
Cow'rs down, and dozes till the dawn of day,
Then claps his well-fledg'd wings and bears away.

F I N I S.

Lately publifhed, a New Edition, Price 2d. or 9s. a Hundred.

A N
E P I S T L E

TO A

GENTLEMAN of the TEMPLE,

Occafioned by *Two Treatifes*, wherein the *Fall of Man*
is differently reprefented, *viz.*

I. Mr. LAW's *Spirit* of *Prayer.*
II. The Bifhop of LONDON's *Appendix,*

SHEWING,

That, according to the plaineft Senfe of SCRIPTURE, the *Nature*
of the *Fall* is greatly miftaken in the latter.

Printed for G. ROBINSON, PATER-NOSTER ROW,

Where may be had, Mr. Law's Works compleat, in 9 Vo-
lumes Octavo, Price 2l. 5s. bound; or any of his Pieces
feparate, fome of which may be had gratis.